Special thanks to Linda Chapman

To Ellie King, a magical friend

ORCHARD BOOKS
338 Euston Road, London NW1 3BH
Orchard Books Australia
Level 17/207 Kent Street, Sydney, NSW 2000
A Paperback Original

First published in 2014 by Orchard Books

Text © Hothouse Fiction Limited 2014

Illustrations © Orchard Books 2014

A CIP catalogue record for this book is available
from the British Library.

ISBN 978 1 40832 903 0

3 5 7 9 10 8 6 4 2

Printed in Great Britain

Orchard Books is a division of Hachette Children's Books,
an Hachette UK company

www.hachette.co.uk

Series created by Hothouse Fiction
www.hothousefiction.com

Rainbow Lion

ROSIE BANKS

ORCHARD

This is the Secret Kingdom

Thunder Castle

Contents

Another Adventure Begins!

"Isn't it sunny?" said Ellie, pushing her red, curly hair back and tilting her face up to the blue sky.

Summer and Jasmine smiled and nodded. The three friends were sitting on the grass in Summer's garden. Their parents were chatting on the patio and Summer's two younger brothers were playing a game with Ellie's little sister, Molly. Smoke from the barbecue drifted around the garden.

A ladybird landed on Summer's hand. She smiled. She loved all animals, even tiny ones!

"You should make a wish," said Jasmine.

Summer shut her eyes. *I wish we could go back to the Secret Kingdom really soon*, she thought. She opened her eyes to find Ellie and Jasmine grinning at her.

"Bet I can guess what you wished for," said Jasmine.

"Could it have something to do with visiting a place with the initials S.K.?" asked Ellie.

"Of course!" Summer smiled.

The three friends shared a wonderful secret. They looked after a beautiful box that could magically transport them to an enchanted land called the Secret Kingdom! They'd had some incredible adventures there and met pixies, elves, mermaids and unicorns, as well as jolly King Merry, the ruler of the kingdom.

The ladybird stretched its wings and flew away.

"I hope my wish comes true," said Summer, watching it go. "The sooner we can go back to the Secret Kingdom the better."

The smiles fell from the others' faces as they nodded. The Secret Kingdom *really* needed their help at the moment. Once every hundred years, four magic animals were released from an enchanted shield – a puppy, a seal, a bird and a lion cub. These were the Animal Keepers, and it was their job to travel around the Secret Kingdom spreading fun, kindness, friendship and courage. When they had been around the whole kingdom, they returned to the shield for another hundred years.

King Merry had invited the girls to watch the Keepers magically appear – but while they had been in the Secret Kingdom, disaster had struck! Queen

Malice, the king's horrible sister, had put a curse on the Animal Keepers so that as they travelled around the land their powers would be reversed – the puppy would make people miserable not happy, the seal would make people mean not kind, the bird would cause people to fight and fall out instead of being friends, and the lion cub would make people cowardly not brave.

The girls had promised to reverse the curse. So far they had managed to find the Puppy Keeper, the Seal Keeper and the Bird Keeper and returned their magic charms to them, breaking the spell. But the Lion Keeper was still somewhere in the Secret Kingdom. They were longing to go back to try and find him!

"Maybe we should see if the Magic

Box has a message for us?" said Ellie, patting her green-and-purple bag. The box was safely inside.

"Okay, but we need to go somewhere private," said Summer. The last thing she wanted was one of her little brothers running over and seeing the box!

"How about your tree house?" suggested Jasmine.

"Good idea," Summer agreed.

The three girls slipped away and climbed up into the tree house. It was shady and cool up there.

"Look, Rosa's here!" said Jasmine, spotting Summer's little black cat. She was curled up on a blanket.

"I was wondering where you were, Rosa," said Summer, stroking the cat's head. Rosa purred happily.

"She seems more cuddly than usual,"
said Ellie with a smile, stroking the cat's
round tummy.

As Rosa stretched, a golden crown-shaped charm on her collar jingled.

Jasmine touched it. "The Lion Keeper's charm," she said softly, thinking about the cute golden lion cub with his rainbow-coloured mane. "If we could just get this charm back on his collar, Queen Malice's curse would be broken!"

Ellie reached into her bag and pulled out the Magic Box. As she put it down on the floor of the treehouse, a bright light sparked across its mirrored lid and then the whole box started to glow and sparkle.

"There's another message for us!" gasped Summer, seeing words swirling across the lid.

Her eyes sparkling with excitement, Ellie read the message out loud:

"To find the lion you must fly
To grasslands lit by a golden sky.
Trouble awaits, be brave not weak,
And find the Keeper that you seek."

The box opened. The magical map
that was stored inside floated up out of
its compartment and hovered in the air
between the girls.

Summer grinned happily as she looked at the glowing pictures. They could see mermaids splashing in the sea, dream dragons sleeping in their valley and tiny pixies swooping around the flying school on magic leaves.

"We need to find somewhere with grass and a golden sky," said Jasmine, her eyes darting across the map.

"Here!" Ellie said, spotting a large plain of tall, waving grass. She read the label. "Golden Grasslands! I bet that's it!"

The girls nodded and all put their hands on the box. "Golden Grasslands!" they cried.

Suddenly a ball of light whizzed out of the box and zoomed around their heads. Rosa sat up with a startled mew. The light disappeared with a faint *pop*,

revealing a tiny
pixie standing
on a green
leaf! She was
wearing a
little safari suit
with matching
boots and had a
hat perched
jauntily
on her
blonde hair.
"Hello,
girls!" she cried.
"Trixi!" they all
exclaimed. Trixibelle was King Merry's
royal pixie and their good friend.

"It's great to see you," said Trixi. "We
must head to the kingdom straight away!"

We're almost out of time before the
Keepers are due to return to their shield.
If we don't find the Lion Keeper, the
whole kingdom will be cowardly forever
thanks to his mixed-up magic! King
Merry and I think he might be in the
Golden Grasslands."

"Let's go right away!" said Summer,
scooping up Rosa.

Trixi smiled and tapped her pixie ring.

"To the grasslands – let's not be late.
Please take us now, no time to waste!"

A whirlwind of red, gold and orange
sparkles blew up out of nowhere. The
girls felt themselves rising up into the air
as if they were as light as dandelion fluff.
As Summer whirled around and around,

excitement bubbled up inside her. They were off on another adventure!

The Golden Grasslands

The girls twirled downwards and their feet hit soft grass.

"Wow!" breathed Jasmine, opening her eyes. It was like arriving in the middle of a wildlife documentary set in Africa; only the sky was yellow and red and orange. The grasslands gleamed golden in the light and in the distance a deep blue pool glinted invitingly. Everywhere seemed to shimmer with magic.

Ellie put her hand to her head and
felt a delicate golden tiara. She smiled.
Whenever they came to the Secret
Kingdom a tiara would appear on each
of their heads, showing everyone in the
kingdom that they were Very Important
Friends of King Merry.

"Look!" cried Summer, pointing to a
nearby tuft of grass. Three very small
animals were standing up on their hind
legs, poking their heads up over the top
of the grass. They looked a bit like tiny
meerkats with big eyes and front paws
tucked close to their chests. Their fur
was a deep, rich red colour and they had
long fluffy tails, like squirrels.

"Aren't they cute!" Summer breathed.

The animals turned to one another.
"Bop bop!" one said.

"Bop bop bop!" said another anxiously.

"BOP!" shrieked the third, and then they all dived down among the grasses and disappeared into a burrow.

"What are they called?" Ellie said.

"They're called bop-bops," explained Trixi. "Because of the noise they make."

"I can hear more of them!" said Jasmine, swinging round as she heard a chorus of "bop-bops" from behind her.

Four more bop-bops were staring at them.

"Bop bop!"

"Bop bop bop BOP!" they chattered, before disappearing down a hole.

Rosa struggled in Summer's arms but Summer kept hold of her. Rosa was very friendly but the bop-bops already seemed quite anxious and Summer didn't want to make them even more worried.

Trixi looked concerned. "The bop-bops seem very nervous today." She flew up into the sky and peered around in all directions. "And there's no sign of any of the other animals."

"What other animals normally live here?" asked Summer.

Trixi smiled at Summer. "Well, there are the jangasnoodles – they're a bit like

the dodos that used to live in your world
but even bigger and a bit bad-tempered.
And there are the kakuras, they look
like wooly mammoths but they are the
same size as sheep and their fur changes
colour." The little pixie sighed. "Where
can they all be?"

"It's a shame we can't talk to the bop-
bops," said Ellie thoughtfully. "Maybe
they know what's been going on."

Jasmine gasped. "What about the
unicorn horn from the Magic Box? That
lets us talk to animals. If we could get
the box here, Trixi, maybe we could use
the horn?"

Trixi quickly tapped her ring:

"Magic Box we need you here.
Please come now, re-appear!"

There was a flash of golden light and
the Magic Box appeared on the grass in
front of them. It opened and the silver
unicorn horn – a gift from the leader of
the unicorns – gleamed in the sunlight.
Ellie carefully lifted it out and the
unicorn horn floated out
in between them.
The girls all held
hands. They
had to all be
touching for
the magic
to work!

A moment
later, the girls
realised they
could hear the
bop-bops chatting in

squeaky voices.

"*Did you see that box?*"

"*Poof! It just appeared.*"

"*Who are the strangers?*"

"*Are they friends?*"

"*They could be enemies. I don't like the look of that furry one!*"

"We're not enemies!" Ellie burst out. "We're friends of King Merry's."

"And this is Rosa," said Summer. "She won't hurt you."

The bop-bops squeaked in alarm and disappeared.

"Please come back," Summer said gently. We want to talk to you."

They heard little whispers.

"You do it, Smudge! You talk to them!"

"Yes, go on! You're the bravest."

A small bop-bop poked his head up. He had a black mark in the centre of his forehead. "Can…can you really understand us, strangers?" he asked.

"Yes," said Jasmine. "But only because of this magic horn. Please talk to us! We want to know what's going on. Where have all the other animals gone?"

There was a pause and then, one by one, the other bop-bops poked their heads out.

"Tell them! Tell them what happened!" several of the other bop-bops chattered.

"It was this morning," Smudge said slowly. "Everything was normal and then suddenly a cold wind blew across the grasslands."

"We never get cold winds here," added another bop-bop.

"It wasn't just cold – it made everyone feel scared," said Smudge. "Like something really bad was about to happen. Then we all heard a loud roar. The other animals were terrified and ran away."

"We just dived into our burrows," said another bop-bop.

"We hid inside all morning," Smudge went on. "Do you know what's happening? Why do we all feel so scared?"

Jasmine kneeled down next to the cute little creatures. "Queen Malice has put a curse on the Animal Keepers and their good magic has been mixed up. It sounds like the Lion Keeper has been here and his magic has made everyone feel frightened."

Suddenly a loud cackle rang out across the grasslands and echoed around in a very spooky way.

The bop-bops dived back into their holes. Jasmine quickly put the tiny unicorn horn into her pocket for safekeeping as the Magic Box disappeared. She spun around with Ellie,

Summer and Trixi, and the four friends gasped.

Queen Malice was swooping across the grasslands on a thundercloud! Her frizzy hair streamed out behind her and in her bony fingers she held a black staff. She cackled wickedly.

As they looked more closely, the girls

could see that the horrid queen was
chasing the Lion Keeper! The little lion
cub was running this way and that across
the grasslands, but he was panting and
looked very tired.

"We have to help him!" cried Jasmine,
and the three girls started to run towards
the lion. But before they could get
near him the mean queen threw
a net over the Lion Keeper,
trapping him beneath it!
"Aha!" Queen
Malice cried.

"Now I've got you!" She leaped from her thundercloud and fastened a chain to the lion's collar.

"Oh no! She's captured the Lion Keeper!" gasped Jasmine.

The queen cackled with glee and shook the chain at them. "Now I have the Lion Keeper, no one in the kingdom will EVER feel brave again!"

The Queen's Prisoner

The cub's big eyes were full of tears and his bright rainbow mane quickly faded to a dull grey colour as he stood next to Queen Malice. Summer felt fear grip her insides.

"The Lion Keeper is mine!" crowed the queen. "Soon *I* shall be the only brave person in the kingdom! With everyone feeling scared it'll be easy for me to

throw my ridiculous brother off the
throne. I shall rule the Secret Kingdom at
last!" Her eyes flashed triumphantly.

"No…no, you won't. We're…
we're not going to let you win, Queen
Malice!" Jasmine said, her voice
trembling. Summer hugged Rosa and
looked around. Ellie was biting her nails.
Trixi was hiding behind Ellie. They all
looked petrified!

Of course, Summer realised suddenly. *The lion usually makes everyone feel brave. We're feeling scared because we're near to him and his magic is all mixed up!*

Queen Malice sneered at the girls. "I'm not going to waste any more time chatting with you pathetic creatures. Now that I have the lion, I'm going to travel all around the kingdom making everyone cowardly!"

Cackling to herself, the queen muttered a spell. A ball of green light flew out of the staff and hit the lion cub. For a moment his whole body glowed with green light and then he started to grow. He grew bigger and bigger until he was the size of a fully-grown lion!

The queen vaulted onto his back.

"Onwards!" she shrieked. "We will make everyone in this kingdom too scared to do anything!" She dug her pointy boots into the lion's side. He roared sadly and bounded away into the distance with Queen Malice kicking him on.

"Now what are we going to do?" asked Jasmine in dismay.

"Give up?" said Trixi sadly, her leaf drooping.

"No!" said Summer. "I feel like giving up too, but that's just because of Queen Malice's spell."

"We've got to fight against feeling scared," said Ellie. "We mustn't give in."

Trixi took a deep breath. "Yes, you're right. We've beaten Queen Malice lots of times before."

"But how?" said Jasmine, nervously chewing a fingernail.

"Well," Ellie said. "I guess we need to get the Lion Keeper back so we can put the charm on his collar. As soon as we do that, the queen's curse will break and he'll be back to normal."

"If his charm is like the other Keepers', a summoning spell will appear if we start doing brave things," said Summer. She looked around. "But what can we do?"

The grasslands were empty. The bop-bops had disappeared again and there were no other creatures anywhere. How could they possibly do something brave on a deserted grassy plain?

"Maybe we need to go somewhere else," suggested Jasmine.

Ellie nodded. "Somewhere where we can do something very brave."

"Where's the scariest place in the Secret Kingdom, Trixi?" asked Jasmine.

Trixi shivered. "That's easy – Thunder Castle. There are Storm Sprites and stink toads there and it's *very* dark and creepy."

"Oh," said Summer in a small voice.

"It does sound very scary," said Ellie.

Jasmine took a deep breath. "But we would be doing something really brave if we went there. And we have be *really* brave if we're to make the words appear on the charm and call the Lion Keeper back to us!"

Ellie and Summer nodded. Neither of them liked the idea, but they had to do everything they could to help the last Animal Keeper and make everyone in the kingdom happy and brave again!

"Will you be able to take us to Thunder Castle with your magic, Trixi?" Ellie asked.

"Y—yes," Trixi stuttered, not sounding like she wanted to go at all. But suddenly her ring started to glow. She gasped.

"Wait! King Merry is trying to get in touch with me."

A moment later, the girls heard King Merry's voice echoing through the air.

"Trixi! What's happening? Where are you?" The king usually sounded very cheerful but now his voice was worried and scared.

Trixi spoke into the ring. "I'm in the Golden Grasslands, Your Majesty. With Jasmine, Summer and Ellie. We've just seen—"

"Oh, Trixi! I'm

feeling so frightened and lonely," the
king interrupted. "I'm hiding under my
duvet! Please come back and keep me
company!"

Trixi looked torn. "But Your Majesty,
the girls and I need to go to Thunder
Castle—"

"Thunder Castle," quavered the king.
"Why do you want to go to that horrible
place?"

"Oh, Sire. I've got terrible news!" Trixi
quickly explained about their encounter
with Queen Malice and the Lion Keeper.
The girls heard King Merry gulp.

"Oh, crowns and castles! This is
terrible, just terrible! Well, there's nothing
else for it. If you're all going to be so
brave, then I must be brave too! I shall
use the rainbow slide to come and meet

you right away and we can all go to Thunder Castle together. I'll be there in the shake of a peacock's tail!"

"Is King Merry coming here?" asked Summer as the ring stopped glowing.

"Yes." Trixi looked worried. "But if he's with us, who will guard the Keepers' Shield at the palace? Queen Malice mustn't get her hands on it. The other three Keepers are still travelling around the kingdom, spreading their good magic, and if the queen gets the shield they'll all be under her control!"

Just then Rosa gave an alarmed mew as a ball of rainbow-coloured light appeared in front of them. It spun round and round, getting bigger and bigger until it became as big as the mouth of a tunnel.

The girls gasped as brightly coloured
sparks shot off it and then, with a
whoosh, King Merry came flying out!
He landed with a bump at their feet.
He was clutching the golden
shield to his chest.

There were four blurry pictures on the front of the shield – the girls could just make out the shapes of a puppy, a bird, a seal and the lion cub. King Merry blinked and looked round. His crown was hanging down over his face and his curly white hair was even messier than usual!

"King Merry!" cried Ellie.

"Are you all right, Your Majesty?" said Trixi, zooming round his head on her leaf.

"Right as rain, Trixi," said King Merry, adjusting his crown. "It was just a bit of a bumpy landing. How lovely to see you, my dear friends," he said as Ellie and Jasmine helped him up and Summer handed him his glasses. "And my favourite puss-cat!" he added, spotting Rosa.

"It's lovely to see you too, King Merry," Summer said, and Rosa gave a loud purr in agreement.

"And you brought the shield!" exclaimed Jasmine. King Merry nodded. The shield was so big, the tubby little king could barely see over the top of it.

"I couldn't risk leaving it behind. But how we're going to carry it with us to Thunder Castle, I just don't know."

"I think I can solve that problem, Your Majesty!" said Trixi. She tapped her ring. There was a bright flash of light and suddenly the shield was no bigger than Trixie's leaf!

"You're a marvel, Trixi. I don't know what I'd do without you," King Merry said, smiling warmly at the little pixie.

Trixi blushed and looked very pleased.

The king tucked the tiny shield inside his cloak. "So, we're really off to Thunder Castle?" he said. He swallowed nervously. "It's very frightening there."

"We have to go. We need to be as brave as we can to make the summoning spell appear on the lion's charm," explained Ellie.

"We'll be all right as long as we stick together," said Summer. Her stomach was turning somersaults but she knew they had to stick to their plan.

Jasmine took a deep breath. "We can beat Queen Malice. I know we can," she said, trying to sound braver than she felt.

"Is everyone ready?" asked Trixi.

They all nodded nervously. Trixi tapped her ring and the girls felt themselves spinning away. They were off to Thunder Castle!

Storm Sprite Guards!

The girls and King Merry landed on rocky ground. They were standing just inside the creeper-covered walls of Thunder Castle. The castle loomed in front of them, tall and forbidding. The girls had seen the outside of the castle once before, and it was just as scary as they remembered! Black flags flew from its spiky battlements and the sky overhead was a strange purple colour, like a bruise. It was the loneliest place imaginable! Fear pressed down on the girls like a heavy blanket and Jasmine shrank backwards. Usually nothing scared her, but now all she wanted to do was run away. She swallowed hard and put her hands up to straighten her tiara.

As soon as her fingers touched the golden crown, she felt warmth flood through her, calming her down. Pictures of all the adventures they'd had in the Secret Kingdom sped through her mind. They'd always beaten Queen Malice in the past. They couldn't let her horrible spell get the better of them this time!

Jasmine looked at Summer and Ellie. "We can do this," she told them. "I know we can. Touch your tiaras.

It'll make you feel better."

They did as she said and they both
breathed out a sigh. "You're right," said
Ellie. "We *can* be brave enough. We
have to do this for the Secret Kingdom!"

Summer saw that King Merry's face
was still pale. Trixi was perched on his
shoulder, shivering. Summer went over
and hugged the king. "It'll be all right,
King Merry," she told him.

He looked into her eyes and managed a shaky smile. "Swords and sceptres. You're right, my dear. We just all have to be brave together."

"So, how are we going to get in?" said Ellie, looking up the hill towards the castle. The huge door was shut and all the windows were barred.

"Can you magic us inside, Trixi?" Jasmine asked.

Trixi shook her head. "Queen Malice has put spells of protection on the castle walls so that no one can get in using magic." She looked round uneasily. "And we must watch out for the Storm Sprites. They guard the castle grounds."

"Let's head for the door and see if we can find a way in," suggested Ellie.

But as she spoke, they heard the sound

of flapping wings overhead. "I'm sure
I heard voices!" a harsh voice called.
"Over this way!"

"There's nothing here," grumbled
another voice. "You're a slug brain!"

"With cabbages for ears!" sniggered a
third voice.

"It's the Storm Sprites!" squeaked Trixi
in alarm. "Quick everyone – hide!"

Everyone dived
behind the curtain
of creepers that
hung down from
the castle walls.
Summer
picked up
Rosa and
pulled her in
with them.

They all huddled together, holding their breath. Summer tried to keep Rosa as far away from the king as possible so he wouldn't sneeze! King Merry loved cats but he was very allergic to them.

The three Storm Sprites flew closer. They had grey pointed faces and leathery wings like giant bats.

"I'm sure the voices came from somewhere round here!" said the first one, landing on the grass where the friends had just been standing.

"There's no one here. You made it up!" said one. "I want my supper!"

"I don't know why," grumbled another. "It's only worm pie again. Queen Malice is mean. She never gives us anything yummy like cake!"

"You'll be lucky to even get worm pie if intruders get into Thunder Castle," the first Storm Sprite said. "You know she said we had to watch out for those pesky girls."

"Well, I can't see any girls here," grumbled the second. "You're imagining things, slime brain!"

"Am not, beetle nose!"

"So are, maggot ears!"

"I heard something. I tell you I did!" insisted the first one. "Come on, let's keep looking."

Grumbling and arguing, the sprites flapped away.

Behind the curtain of creepers, Ellie let out a trembling breath. "They've gone!"

"Goodness gracious me, that was close," said King Merry, wiping his forehead.

"How are we going to get inside the castle with them patrolling the grounds?" whispered Summer, clutching Rosa.

"We need to distract them," said Jasmine.

They all thought hard, but it was difficult to come up with ideas when they felt so jumpy and afraid!

"I know," said Ellie slowly. "The sprites are very greedy. Trixi, would you be able to magic up a big cake that contains a sleeping spell? Then they'd eat it and go to sleep."

"Brilliant idea!" whispered Jasmine. "We could even put a note on it saying it's from Queen Malice to reward her loyal servants!"

Summer blinked. "Surely even the Storm Sprites aren't stupid enough to believe that?"

Jasmine grinned. "Only one way to find out!"

"I'll put the cake over there so we can see what's happening," whispered Trixi, pointing a little way off.

Summer scanned the dark sky. "Be quick! They could come back at any time." Her heart was thudding against her ribs.

Trixi zoomed off on her leaf. She stopped a little way off from their hiding place and tapped her ring. There was a flash and a giant cake appeared! It had ten tiers and was decorated in purple icing with silver balls all over it.

At the top of it there was a sugar lightning bolt and a note.

Trixi whizzed back to the girls. "I've done it!"

Just then the friends heard bickering voices heading back towards them.

"There was a flash over here! I saw something. I did!"

The girls, King Merry and Trixi quickly jumped back behind the curtain of creepers. Ellie could feel fear prickling her skin. What if the Storm Sprites realised it was a trick?

Jasmine gripped her hand. Her eyes were wide and scared. Beside her King Merry was holding his nose in case he sneezed and gave their hiding place away.

"Look!" shrieked the first sprite,

spotting the cake. "I told you I saw something!"

"What is it?" said the second sprite curiously. "It looks like a...a..."

"A cake!" they all cried.

Peering out from behind the ivy, the girls saw the sprites flap down to investigate.

"It's from Queen Malice," said one, picking up the note and reading it out. "*To my loyal servants, a reward for guarding my castle so well!*"

Trixi winked at the girls. Ellie felt very anxious. She hoped the trick worked!

One of the sprites puffed his chest out. "Well, obviously we are the best guards *ever!*"

"And we absolutely deserve cake," said another.

"Of course we do!" crowed the third. "We're the best!"

Jasmine nudged Summer. "Told you!" she mouthed. Summer felt a rush of relief. The Storm Sprites might be a bit scary, but they really weren't very clever! They started digging into the cake.

"Yummy yummy cake!" said the first, grabbing a huge handful.

"Oi, you greedy guzzler!

Don't eat my share!" said the second.

"Or mine!" said the third, cramming icing and sponge into his mouth. "It's delicious, it's amazing, it's…" His voice trailed off and he suddenly flopped to the ground, fast asleep!

The other two sprites sank down too. One even started sucking his thumb!

They all snored loudly in unison.

"You did it, Trixi!" whispered Summer in delight.

They jumped out of their hiding place. Summer put Rosa down. The charm jingled as the cat shook herself, catching Summer's eye.

"The charm is glowing!" she cried. "And some of the spell has appeared!"

"What does it say?" asked Jasmine.

Summer read the words out:

"These words will call me without fail,
From sea or mountain..."

"It's working! We just need to carry on doing brave things," Summer said. "Then the rest of it should appear." She looked at the others. "Let's head inside the castle."

They all crept up the path towards the castle door. It was made of dark wood and had serpents carved onto it and a lightning bolt for a handle.

"Do you think it will be open?" Ellie whispered hopefully.

"I doubt it," said King Merry, puffing slightly from climbing up the hill. "My sister hates the thought of anyone being

able to get in without her permission."

Ellie tried to turn the handle but the door wouldn't open. "You're right, it's locked," she sighed.

Jasmine bit her lip. "So what are we going to do now? We need to get inside before the Storm Sprites wake up!"

Brave Best Friends

"Maybe there's another door somewhere?" suggested Summer. "One that isn't locked."

They started to hunt around the castle walls but there were no other doors, only windows, and they were all tightly shut and barred.

Rosa trotted along beside them. A rat darted out from behind a tuft of grass and she started to chase it. "Rosa!

Come back!" called Summer, but the cat ignored her. Summer hurried after her. "Rosa!"

The rat suddenly disappeared and Rosa gave a surprised mew. Catching up with her, Summer saw that the rat had vanished into a small tunnel, leading underground. "Look at this!" Summer said, beckoning the others over.

They crowded round. "What is it?" said Jasmine.

King Merry shuddered. "I think I know. It's a way for my sister's pet stink toads to get in and out of the castle. They like to swim in the moat and sleep in the slimy dungeons."

As he spoke, a horrible smell of rotten eggs wafted through the air. Everyone wrinkled their noses as a stink toad squeezed its warty body out through the gap under the wall. It gave them a haughty look and hopped off down the hill.

Jasmine watched it go. On one of their other adventures, King Merry had come dangerously close to being turned into a stink toad. She was very glad they had stopped the wicked queen that time. *And we can stop her again*! she told herself as firmly as she could.

The others were looking back at the tunnel. "It's a way in!" said Summer excitedly. "But none of us apart from Trixi could fit through there."

"Unless we all became the same size as Trixi!" said Jasmine. Her eyes lit up. "Trixi, could you use your magic to make us small enough to fit into the tunnel?"

"That's a wonderful idea!" cried King Merry as Trixi nodded.

"Wait," said Ellie suddenly. "Trixi, I

thought you said Queen Malice had put a spell on the castle so people can't use magic to get in?"

"Yes, she has, but the spell is on the castle *walls*!" said Trixi, looking excited. "And we'd be going *underneath* them. I really think it might work!" She spun round in the air on her leaf. "Shall we try it?"

The dark tunnel looked scary but they knew they had to get inside the castle. "Yes!" they all said at once.

Trixi tapped her ring.

"Big friends become small like me.
Travel underground using lights to see!"

There was a green flash of light and
everyone shrank to pixie size – even
Rosa! Trixi had also magicked little
lanterns for them to hold.

Jasmine walked forwards to the mouth of the tunnel. "It's quite scary in here!" she called shakily, making her way slowly into the darkness.

Trixi swooped in after her and the king hurried after Trixi, rubbing his hands together nervously.

Summer looked at Ellie. Neither of them had moved.

"I guess we should go too." Summer didn't like the dark and the thought of walking through the gloomy, smelly tunnel was very scary indeed!

"Yes." Ellie swallowed, trying to be brave. "We've got our lanterns. And we'll all be together."

Holding hands, they both made their way over to the entrance of the tunnel. It was cold and damp inside with slimy, rocky walls. It would have been pitch black, but their lanterns lit up the gloom.

Jasmine was waiting for them, looking round uneasily. "I hope we don't meet any spiders!" She shuddered.

"I don't mind spiders. I'll lead the way," said Trixi. "Follow me!"

She set off through the tunnel, flying slowly so the girls and King Merry could keep up. The tunnel twisted and turned until it reached a large underground

corridor. Set into the walls were several heavy-looking metal doors, with bars at the windows. Candles were flickering faintly in the gloomy light.

"My sister's dungeons!" said King Merry, looking around and shaking his head in disgust. "I pity any poor prisoners who end up here."

To the girls' relief there didn't seem to be any prisoners in the dungeons' cells, just stink toads hopping about in puddles of water. The smell was revolting!

"Will you change us back now, please, Trixi?" said Ellie.

Trixi tapped her ring. They all felt a fierce rushing sensation and suddenly they were back to normal size. Rosa shook her head and blinked. Her collar jingled.

Summer kneeled down and checked the charm. "More words have appeared!" she said.

"These words will call me without fail,
From sea or mountain, hill or dale.
Say my name, jump off the..."

"It sounds like we just need one more little bit," said Jasmine in excitement. "Then we can call the Lion Keeper!"

"Let's keep going," said Summer, spotting a spiral staircase leading upwards. She touched her tiara and felt another rush of comforting warmth. "Come on!"

They tiptoed up the staircase and into a large entrance hall. It was painted black and red and a very spiky

chandelier hung down from the ceiling.
Ghostly strands of cobwebs hung from
the curtains and another
much grander staircase led
upstairs. The bannisters
were made of twisted metal
and a curtain of cobwebs
draped down from the
ceiling, hiding the first
step.

Ellie felt as if her heart was in her mouth. "Do you think Queen Malice's throne room is up those stairs?"

King Merry nodded. "I'm sure it is."

"You mean we have to go through those cobwebs to get to it?" said Jasmine faintly. "I really don't think I can do that!"

Summer didn't mind spiders, but even she felt her skin prickle at the thought of pushing through the cobwebby curtain.

Suddenly a huge spider ran across the floor. Jasmine squealed and leaped back.

"You'll be okay." Summer took Jasmine's hand. "Spiders can't hurt you. And we'll be right by your side."

Ellie took Jasmine's other hand. "Shut your eyes and just imagine the cobweb is a glitter curtain on a stage."

Jasmine shut her eyes. "I'm trying," she said in a small voice.

"Keep imagining," Summer told her as she and Ellie moved forwards. "We're walking towards the stage. We'll be through the curtains in a moment…the audience is waiting for you…"

Holding tightly to their hands, Jasmine walked through the cobweb. But it stuck to their clothes and got caught in their hair and faces! Summer and Ellie tried to brush the cobwebs away from Jasmine as best they could.

"We're through!" exclaimed Ellie a few moments later.

Jasmine opened her eyes. "I did it!" she said in relief, brushing the remaining strands of cobweb off her hair and top.

But just then a spider appeared right in

front of her! She gave a loud shriek and
backed away.

"Jasmine, look closer!" smiled Summer,
pointing at the spider.

Jasmine reluctantly looked at the spider
again, and saw that it was waving at
her! Jasmine suddenly remembered she
still had the magic unicorn horn in her

pocket. Clutching it in her hand she heard the spider say "Hello"!

She listened carefully to the spider. "You have a nice day too!" she called as he scuttled away.

"What did he say?" asked Summer.

"That it was nice to see visitors here and he wished us a good day."

"See, I told you spiders weren't scary," Summer grinned.

The friends hurried up to the top of the staircase with King Merry and Trixi close behind. In front of them was a huge room with a black spiky throne at one end. Dusty curtains hung beside the windows and stone gargoyles and serpents glared down at them from tall pillars. The ceiling was painted with pictures of snakes and crows.

"Queen Malice's throne room!"
breathed Ellie.

"Check Rosa's collar now," urged
Jasmine. "Surely we've been brave
enough to make the spell appear!"

The friends held their breath as
Summer looked at the glowing charm.
Every single word of the summoning
spell was shining clearly!

"We've done it!" she exclaimed.

"Read the spell out!" urged Ellie.

Summer took the charm from Rosa's
collar. This was the moment they had
been waiting for. Now they could finally
summon the lion and give him his crown
charm back! She read the words out:

"These words will call me without fail,
From sea or mountain, hill or dale.
Say my name, jump off the floor,
Not just once, but times by four."

Jasmine grabbed Ellie and Summer's
hands. "Are you ready?"

They nodded.

"Lion Keeper!" the three girls called out together as they jumped up and down four times.

There was a bright golden flash and the lion appeared in front of them. But the girls gasped in horror. Not only was the Lion Keeper still huge but, even worse, Queen Malice was with him – riding on his back!

The Queen Returns

Queen Malice howled with rage. "How dare you break into my castle and summon the lion!" She flung herself off the lion's back, her black hair sticking up in all directions. "I'm going to teach you girls a lesson you'll never forget! You too, brother!"

She strode towards them all.

"Stop!" cried Trixi, bravely flying up to Queen Malice.

"Get out of my way, you silly pixie!"
The queen batted Trixi away with her
staff, sending her flying through the air.
Jasmine leaped to catch her, and Ellie
and Summer ran at Queen Malice to try
to grab her staff. But Summer bumped
into Ellie and the three girls and Trixi
landed in a tangled heap on the floor!

The queen raised her staff. "So you
think you can stop me, do you? Well,
prepare to be turned into stink toads!"

The queen started to chant a spell:

"Magic dark and magic deep..."

"NO!" thundered King Merry. He
strode forwards. "I will not let you harm
my friends, sister! You will leave these
girls alone!"

"Oh, will I indeed?" jeered Queen
Malice, looking round at him. "I don't
take orders from you, brother!"

King Merry drew himself to his full
height. "I am the king of this land and
you will do as I say!" he shouted in a
voice so loud it made the room shake.

The girls scrambled to their feet and held hands. They had never heard King Merry sound so angry! Even Queen Malice looked alarmed. She took an uncertain step back.

King Merry strode towards her. "This evil will stop now!" he commanded. "You have tried to make everyone in this kingdom unhappy, mean, unfriendly and cowardly. I will *not* put up with it!"

Summer nudged Ellie and Jasmine, her eyes wide. The Lion Keeper's charm had floated out of her hand and was travelling towards the lion!

"Why is it doing that?" whispered Ellie.

"I think the lion's mixed-up magic is reacting to King Merry being so brave!" Summer gasped.

The Lion Keeper's head was drooping

sadly, but when he noticed the charm
whizzing towards him he stretched his
great head out, his ears pricking up
hopefully. There was a bright flash of
golden light as the charm reached
his collar, making the
lion roar in delight.
His dull grey
mane instantly
changed to a
rainbow mix of
colours that shone
and sparkled!

"The curse is broken!" cried Trixi.

The queen looked furious and thumped
her staff on the ground angrily. "So?
It doesn't change things!" she hissed,
spinning around and narrowing her
eyes at the girls. "The lion has already

done his work – everyone in the Secret Kingdom is a coward now. This kingdom is going to be a very different place from now on. I will take over—"

"RRRRRRRRROAR!" the lion interrupted her. He was still big and could roar very loudly!

Jasmine pulled the unicorn horn out of her pocket and grabbed Ellie and Summer's hands. She wanted to hear what the Lion Keeper had to say!

"You're wrong!" the Lion Keeper roared to Queen Malice. "The good magic of the Animal Keepers will undo all of your dark magic. Now we're free from your spell, we will defeat you!"

"Use your magic, Lion Keeper!" King Merry urged. "Show my sister what you can do!"

The lion shook his magnificent mane and there was a bright flash. Suddenly the other three Animal Keepers appeared – the bouncing puppy, the friendly seal and the beautiful bird. They met each other and touched noses. As they did so, a golden light began to spread all around, so dazzling it made the queen cover her eyes.

A hot, brave, happy feeling rushed
through all three girls.

Ellie turned to the others, her green
eyes sparkling. "I feel incredible!"

"Me too," said Jasmine.

"I feel braver than I've ever felt in my
life," said Summer. "And so happy!"

"It's the Keepers' magic!" cried Trixi,
flying a loop-the-loop. "It's making us
feel this way! And it'll do the same to
everyone in the kingdom!"

King Merry laughed in delight.
"Crowns and sceptres, I feel two hundred
years younger!"

"Look at the Storm Sprites!" cried Ellie,
running to the window. The light was
spreading beyond the castle, illuminating
the sky. The sprites had woken up and
were getting to their feet. They turned

their faces to the sky and then started to smile and laugh. One of them even started doing a little jig!

"Nooooo!" shrieked the queen, clutching her head as she stared out of the window.

The lion roared again and charged at her with his mouth open, showing his sharp teeth. He looked very angry!

Queen Malice gave a shriek and started to run away. The lion chased her around the room and the seal joined in. The bird flew around her head and the puppy nipped at her heels. They chased her all the way out of the throne room and down the stairs, yapping, growling, honking and hooting.

"To the dungeons with her, Animal Keepers!" chortled King Merry. "Teach her a lesson! She can stay there while she thinks about what she's done and how much trouble she has caused!"

Summer hugged him. "Oh, King Merry. The curse has lifted and everything's going to be okay after all!"

The king beamed. "Thank you so much, my dear friends. You have saved the Secret Kingdom once again. I don't know what we'd do without you." He looked round. "But someone's missing. Where's my favourite cat?"

They all looked around the throne room. Rosa had disappeared!

"Where's she gone?" Summer said in alarm.

"When did you last see her?" Jasmine asked.

Summer thought hard. "I remember her coming up the stairs with us, but I haven't seen her since. Oh, where can she be!"

"Maybe she got stuck in the cobwebs!" Jasmine said, her eyes widening.

"Let's go and look for her!" said Ellie.

Summer ran to the door. There were tears in her eyes. "Rosa!" she shouted. "Rosa! Where are you?"

Rosa's Surprise!

They all ran around desperately searching for Rosa. The castle seemed much less scary now that the Keepers' golden light was shining through the rooms and corridors, but Summer still hated the thought of her little cat being lost and alone!

Ellie checked in one room, Jasmine in another, while King Merry and Trixi searched the throne room. Summer ran to a door at the far end of the corridor.

It was slightly ajar. Maybe Rosa had gone in there?

As she pushed the door open she realised it must be Queen Malice's bedroom. The walls were covered with black-and-silver tapestries with pictures of scary serpents and gruesome gargoyles. There was a huge four-poster bed in the centre of the room, its posts carved into the shape of lightening bolts. Summer was just about to leave the room when a movement on the bed caught her eye.

"Rosa!" Summer cried, running over. "We've been looking for you! Did you decide to have a little rest—" She broke off with a gasp. Rosa wasn't alone! Snuggled next to her were four tiny, fluffy kittens – each small enough to fit in the palm of Summer's hand. There was

a tabby kitten,
a ginger one,
a tortoiseshell
and a black-
and-white
one! Rosa
purred
loudly as if to
say "Aren't I
clever?"

Just then, Jasmine and Ellie looked into the room.

"Have you found Rosa ?' Ellie asked.

"Y—yes," stammered Summer, almost too shocked to speak. She pointed at the bed.

"Kittens!" gasped Jasmine.

"King Merry! Trixi! Come quick!" cried Ellie in delight.

Summer sat down on the bed and
Rosa purred as she gently stroked the
kittens' heads. Being new-born their eyes
were still closed but they rubbed against
Summer's fingers as she stroked them.
The ginger kitten let out a happy squeak.
They were the most adorable things
Summer had ever seen!

"They're so cute," breathed Ellie as she
and Jasmine gathered round.

King Merry and Trixi came hurrying
in. "What is it? Have you found her?"
puffed the king. "Have you… Oh,
swords and sceptres!" he exclaimed.
"Kittens! Adorable kittens! What a
clever cat!"

"She is," Summer said softly, kissing
Rosa's head. "She's the best cat in the
world!"

Just then, the four Animal Keepers
came bounding, flapping and bouncing
into the room. The girls were very
pleased to see that the lion was back
to his usual cub size, looking very cute
indeed. He growled softly and Trixi
smiled.

"It looks like the last of Queen Malice's magic has worn off! The Lion Keeper says that she's safely shut in the dungeons. They've given her some worm pie to eat if she gets hungry!"

The puppy put his paws over his nose as if he was laughing. The lion shook his mane and the seal clapped her flippers together.

"Your Majesty, I think it's time for the Keepers to go back into their shield now," said Trixi.

"Of course! We need the shield!" King Merry took the tiny shield out from inside his cloak. With a tap of Trixi's ring it grew back to its full size. Trixi tapped her ring again and her outfit changed into an amazing ceremonial robe, complete with feathered hat!

King Merry held the shield steady.
"Thank you, Keepers," he said solemnly.
"Your job here is done for another
hundred years."

The Keepers bounded and fluttered
around the room, saying goodbye to
everyone. The lion cub, seal and puppy
nuzzled the girls' arms and legs, and the
bird rubbed its beak gently against their
cheeks.

"It's been amazing meeting you," said
Ellie.

The four animals bowed their heads
and then ran and flew towards the shield.
All four Keepers vanished in a bright
flash of light. Jasmine blinked and saw
that the pictures on the shield were clear
again – each animal was back in its
rightful place.

"The four Animal Keepers – back where they belong," King Merry said softly.

Summer stroked Rosa and looked at the king. "I should take Rosa and her kittens back to where they belong, too."

"Indeed, Thunder Castle is no place for such sweet little kittens," said King Merry. "They should be snuggled up in their own home."

Summer looked round. "I'm not sure how we're going to carry them home."

"I can help!" Trixi said. There was a bright flash and a beautiful cosy basket with a handle appeared on the bed. It was lined with soft cream fleece.

Summer beamed. "It's perfect! Thank you, Trixi!" She, Ellie and Jasmine gently picked up Rosa and put her in the basket

and then tucked the tiny kittens in beside
her. They squeaked contentedly and
Rosa purred gratefully.

Trixi whispered in King Merry's ear.

"An excellent idea!" he declared. "Trixi
thinks we should give each of the kittens
a gift before they go. Would you like
that?"

"Yes, please!" said Summer.

Trixi tapped her ring and silver sparkles
flew out, surrounding the basket. As
they cleared, Summer saw that each of
the kittens was now wearing a brightly

coloured collar and on each collar there
was a tiny silver charm – the tabby had
a heart, the tortoiseshell had a balloon,
the black-and-white kitten had a flower
and the ginger kitten had a crown.

"They're like the Keepers' collar
charms!" said Jasmine.

Trixi grinned. "Now the kittens will
have a little bit of Secret Kingdom magic
with them always – even when they're in
the human world."

"The collars will grow with the kittens
and bring them good health and good
luck always," said King Merry.

Summer's eyes shone. "Thank you so
much!"

King Merry smiled. "Thank *you* for
all you three have done. Without your
help, Queen Malice would surely rule

the kingdom!" He hugged the three girls tightly. "Now, we must say goodbye."

"But it won't be goodbye for long," Ellie said. "Will it?"

"No." King Merry shook his head and smiled. "I'm sure it won't."

"If you need us, just send us a message," said Jasmine. "We'll be waiting!"

Summer picked up the basket, and Ellie and Jasmine tucked their hands through her elbows. Trixi kissed them each on the nose and tapped her ring. Gold and silver sparkles surrounded the girls and they were lifted up into the air and whisked away!

A moment later they landed back in the treehouse. Down in the garden they could hear their younger brothers and sisters shouting and laughing and the hum of their parents' voices.

"We're back," said Summer, blinking. It always took a few moments to get used to being back in the human world! She smiled happily. Queen Malice had been defeated and their friends in the

Secret Kingdom were safe once again.
And Rosa had four adorable kittens!

The three friends grinned at each other.
The kittens' collar charms sparkled in the
sunlight that was flooding into the tree
house.

"Things feel pretty much perfect," said
Jasmine with a happy sigh.

"I know," smiled Ellie. "I can't wait for
more amazing adventures in the Secret
Kingdom!"

In the next Secret Kingdom adventure, Ellie, Summer and Jasmine meet the

Pixie Princess

Read on for a sneak peek...

Ready for Adventure!

Boing! Boing! Ellie Macdonald, Summer Hammond and Jasmine Smith jumped up and down on the trampoline in Jasmine's back garden. The sun was shining brightly in the clear blue sky.

"This is fun!" cried Ellie, her red curls bouncing around.

"Watch me!" Jasmine tried to turn a

somersault but she ended up in a heap at their feet. "Whoops!"

Giggling, Ellie and Summer flopped down beside her. "It's so warm!" said Summer pushing back her blonde plaits and fanning her face.

Jasmine rolled on to her back. "I feel like I'm going to melt."

Ellie grinned as she thought of a joke. "What do you call a dog on a day like this?"

"What?" the others said.

"A hot dog!" Ellie giggled as Jasmine and Summer both groaned. Ellie had a thought and glanced around to check that Jasmine's mum wasn't near the trampoline. "I wonder if it's this warm in the Secret Kingdom at the moment," she said in a low voice.

"Oh, I wish we could go there to find out!" said Summer longingly.

Jasmine nodded. "I really feel like going on a Secret Kingdom adventure today."

"I feel like going on one *every* day!" Ellie grinned.

The three girls had a very special secret – they were the only people that knew about a magical world called the Secret Kingdom! Ellie smiled as she imagined its lush meadows, rolling hills, tall mountains and sparkling seas. They had made so many friends there – pixies, unicorns, mermaids and elves – as well as the lovely King Merry who ruled the land, and his royal pixie Trixabelle who looked after him. "Do you remember when Trixi made us small and we went to Glitter Bay and helped all the fairies there?" she said.

"Oh, yes," breathed Summer. "It was amazing!"

Ellie sat up. "Why don't we go and check the Magic Box now and see if Trixi's sent us a message? Where is it, Jasmine?"

The girls always took it in turns to look after the Magic Box. At the moment, Jasmine was taking care of it. "It's in my old ballet bag in my wardrobe," Jasmine said. "Come on, we can get a cool drink at the same time."

They jumped off the trampoline and ran into the house. They poured some apple juice into glasses and then went up to Jasmine's bedroom. Her walls were painted a bright pink, she had pretty pink netting over her bed and a stripy pink-and-white duvet cover. On her walls she had stuck up posters of pop stars and actresses and dancers.

"Oh, wouldn't it be brilliant if there was a message for us from Trixi or King Merry?" Jasmine said as she finished her apple juice. Putting the glass down, she opened the wardrobe...

Read

Pixie Princess

to find out what happens next!

Secret Kingdom

Have you read all the books in Series Four?

Meet the magical Animal Keepers of the Secret Kingdom, who spread fun, friendship, kindness and bravery throughout the land!

Secret Kingdom

Be in on the secret... Discover the first enchanting series!

Series 1

When Jasmine, Summer and Ellie discover the magical land of the Secret Kingdom, a whole world of adventure awaits!

Secret Kingdom

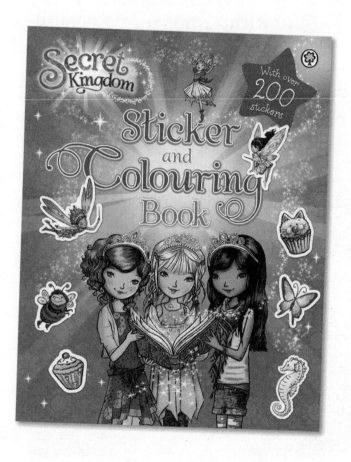

The magical world of Secret Kingdom comes to life with this gorgeous sticker and colouring book. Out now!

Look out for the next sparkling summer special!

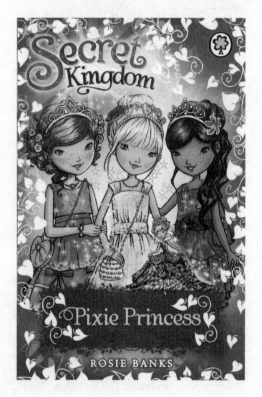

Join the girls on a special pixie-sized adventure!

Available
June 2014

Secret Kingdom

Don't miss the next amazing series!

It's Ellie, Summer and Jasmine's most
important adventure yet... Queen Malice has
taken over the Secret Kingdom! The girls must
find four magic jewels to make King Merry
a new crown and return him to the throne –
but where in the kingdom can the gems be?

Available
August 2014

Secret Kingdom Shield Competition!

Can you help best friends
Ellie, Summer and Jasmine solve the riddles?

At the back of each Secret Kingdom adventure in this set (books 19–22) is a different riddle for you to solve. The answers are all connected to a character featured in this set of Secret Kingdom books.

Here's how you enter the competition:

✳ Read and solve the riddle on the page opposite

✳ Once you think you know the answer, go to
www.secretkingdombooks.com
to print out the special shield activity sheet

✳ Draw the animal that you think is the answer
to the riddle on the shield

✳ Once you've drawn all four correct answers,
send your entry into us!

The lucky winners will receive a bumper Secret Kingdom goody bag full of treats and activities.

Please send entries to:
Secret Kingdom Shield Competition
Orchard Books, 338 Euston Road, London, NW1 3BH

Don't forget to add your name and address.

Good luck!

Closing date: 31st October 2014

Riddle four

At Thunder Castle
behind a great wall,

Find the Keeper
that roars, he's not
scary at all!

The answer is

....

Secret Kingdom

A magical world of
friendship and fun!

Join the Secret Kingdom Club at

www.secretkingdombooks.com

and enjoy games, sneak peeks and lots more!

You'll find great activities, competitions, stories
and games, plus a special newsletter for
Secret Kingdom friends!